Mack and Will

by Jane Simon   illustrated by Jill Newton

Orlando   Boston   Dallas   Chicago   San Diego

Visit *The Learning Site!*

www.harcourtschool.com

Printed in China

ISBN 0-15-325493-9

12 13 14 15 16 17 18 19 20   121   10 09 08 07 06 05

Ordering Options
ISBN 0-15-325468-8 (Collection)
ISBN 0-15-326571-X (package of 5)

Mack has a little house.
It is a hole in the hill.
Mack likes his house.

2

Will has a big house.
It is in the town.
Will likes his house.

Mack has a little food.
It is nuts and seeds.
Mack likes his food.

Will has lots of food.
It is cakes and ham.
Will likes his food.

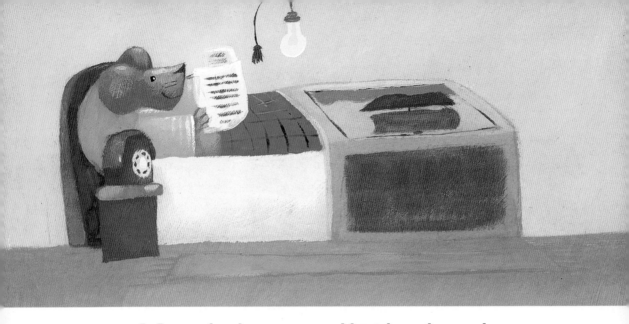

Mack has a little bed.
It is a box.
Mack likes his bed.

Will has a big bed.
It is soft and wide.
Will likes his bed.

Every night, Will calls Mack.
"Good night, Mack," says Will.
"Good night, Will," says Mack.